Coyote  Sto

The Princess
IS BRAVE

To Evie & Jaina

Jeremy Koehn

written and illustrated by
Jeremy L Koehn

465 W Ivyglen St. #240

Mesa, AZ 85201

Manufactured in the United States of America

The illustrations are computer generated images reproduced in full color.

ISBN:9781792750182

www.coyotestory.com

For my sweet little angel Aleithia,

I love you,

Daddy

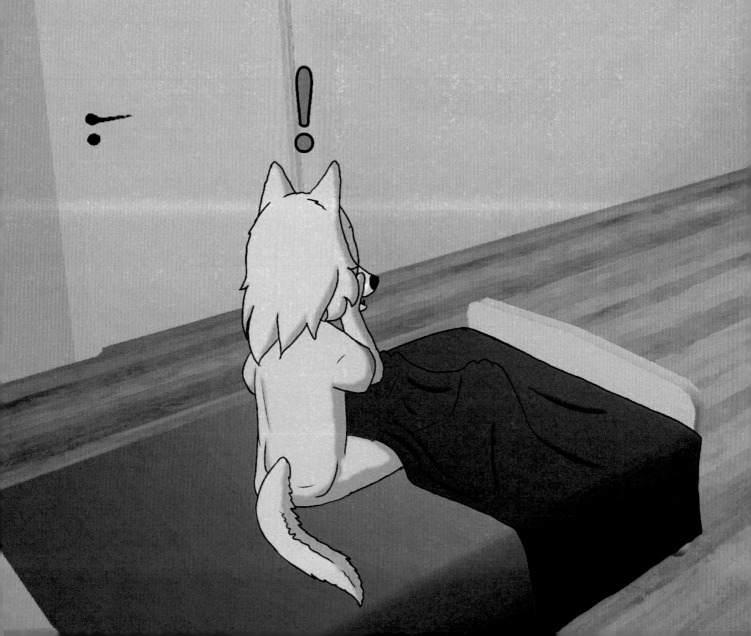

Chassie woke up to to a flash of lightning that caused a scary shadow to appear on her bedroom wall.

"Daddy!" She cried in a loud voice, and Daddy coyote made his way to her room.

"What's wrong sweety? Are you ok?" Asked Daddy. Chassie started to cry. "I'm afraid Daddy, please don't leave!"

Then Chassie begged,
"Please let me sleep
in your room Daddy,
I'm so scared!"
Daddy coyote sighed
and said,
"Sweetheart, I know
you're scared, but
have you ever heard
the story about the
brave princess?"
"No." She replied.

Chassie laid back down and her Daddy sat on a chair and began, "There was once a brave princess who loved her Daddy very much."

He taught her many skills like climbing,

shooting arrows,

and sword fighting.

One dreadful day monsters broke into the castle and grabbed the Princess and the king.

They put the king in the dungeon,

and threw the Princess in the tower. But just before the monster closed the door, a little bird named Ren flew in.

"Rosie, I'm so glad to see you, and you brought my bow and arrows! Thanks Ren!" Said the Princess. "Now let's go find my brothers."

They searched across the kingdom for the Princess' brothers until Rosie spotted them deep in the Fearful Forest. "What on earth are my brothers doing in the Fearful Forest?" Wondered the Princess.

The Princess was really upset.
"Why are you hiding in the Fearful.
Forest? Don't you know Daddy.
needs our help?
Now quit being afraid
and let's go rescue.
Daddy!
She shouted.

"Those monsters don't stand a chance against us!" Said the Princess. But her brothers said, "I Don't know about that, have you seen their claws and sharp teeth?"

When they reached the castle door, the monsters came out to meet them. As soon as the door opened, the Princess reached for an arrow and yelled, "Charge!" When her brothers saw her bravery, they drew their swords and followed her.

The monsters were so suprised that they turned around in fear and ran back inside! The Princess and her brothers chased them all through the castle. Finally, they escaped out the back and ran straight into the Fearful Forest, never to be seen again.

After defeating the monsters, the Princess ran straight to the dungeon. She found her Daddy and wrapped her arms around him.
"Daddy, we beat the monsters and saved the castle!" She shouted
Then her Daddy said, "I'm so proud of all of you, especially you my brave little princess."

"And that's the story of the brave princess," said Daddy coyote, unaware that Chassie was now sound asleep. When he saw her, he smiled, got up, and whispered in her ear,

Made in the USA
San Bernardino, CA
22 January 2019